Metamorphosis

Metamorphosis

FRANZ KAFKA

Illustrated by Gaby Verdooren

SIRIUS

SIRIUS

This edition published in 2024 by Sirius Publishing, a division of
Arcturus Publishing Limited,
26/27 Bickels Yard, 151–153 Bermondsey Street,
London SE1 3HA

ISBN: 978-1-3988-4354-7
AD011826UK

Printed in China

CONTENTS

INTRODUCTION

From Ovid's *Metamorphoses* to Marvel Comics' *X-Men*, it's hard to think of a shape-shifting story that isn't both violent and sensational. None is weirder or more wonderful than Franz Kafka's *Metamorphosis*, but Kafka's story is also richly comic. Born in Prague in 1883, Kafka grew up in a German-speaking family. He wrote the funny, poignant and unsettling *Metamorphosis* in 1912, creating a key text in the revolutionary spirit of 20th-century Modernism – and a classic of surrealist horror.

Metamorphosis tells the story of Gregor Samsa, a successful young travelling salesman who one day wakes to find that he has turned into 'a kind of giant bug'. Kafka's detailed description, of 'the arch of a brown abdomen, divided into stiff, domed segments... [and] a regiment of puny legs', conjures up something between a centipede and a cockroach.

Is the transformation a real, physical fact, or are we meant to understand it on some more profound level, a continuation of the 'troubled dreams' from which young Gregor has just woken? As the anti-hero himself states, 'It was no dream.' And Kafka's painfully funny and extremely realistic depiction of the bug-human struggling to get its ugly, ungainly carapace out of bed asks us to take the transformation at face value.

Any translator coming to Kafka's work sees at once that it is written in clear and concise language whose economy is a clever artistic counterpoint to the subtlety of its underlying themes. Sticking to this plain elegance without taking too many liberties with the original has been the overriding objective of this translation, but the close reader will find that there are a few well-intentioned minor departures.

Despite the disturbing strangeness of events, Kafka's powerful narrative manages to make us suspend disbelief, but at the same time the story works on a deeper level.

If Gregor's plight is a metaphor for the human condition, then how should we interpret it? Stuck in a 15-mile motorway tailback, or in voice-mail jail on the phone to an impenetrable utility company, we all know what it feels like to be Kafka's beetle. He has hit on something universal in human experience. Sadly, for a long time Gregor himself remains in denial about his fall from grace.

This is all the more poignant in that until the horror comes upon him, the young man has been a model of virtue: for several years, ever since his valetudinarian father's business failed, he has singlehandedly supported his parents and teenage sister, Grete. Sweet-natured to a fault – it really doesn't do to be too submissive in life – Samsa's first fear is not for himself, as might be expected, but that, having missed the five a.m. train, his bullying boss will sack him.

As he worries about losing his job, we learn that in fact Gregor hates his work. Is work the metaphoric beetle – the cockroach we all have to bear (unless we happen to enjoy our employment)? If so, it would again strike a pretty universal chord.

In fact, its critique of work is only the first in many levels of understanding that begin to unfold in Kafka's story. Next, he leads us to think about the truculence of youth, and the way in which family power can shift away from parents as their children come into their own. For a short while, Gregor and sister Grete, who takes charge of her bug-brother, enjoy a new and unaccustomed power as their parents struggle and fail to deal with the filthy, crawling nightmare in the bedroom beyond.

Now we have struck the mother lode of Kafka's metaphor – power. The theme will carry us much further, helped on its way by the author's repeated use of brilliant and sinister farce. The office manager comes to find out why Gregor is not at work. Afraid the man will leave before he can explain himself, and quite forgetting he is now a giant bug, the Gregor-monster panics. 'The manager had to be stopped, calmed, convinced and finally won over. His own and his family's future depended on it!... The manager was already on the stairs... Gregor sprang forward to try and stop him. The manager must have guessed what was coming, for he leapt down the steps in a single bound and vanished with a cry of "Aaagh!"... His rapid escape had the unfortunate effect of causing Gregor's father... to fly completely off the handle... he seized the manager's walking stick in his right hand... grabbed a large newspaper from the table to his left and began stamping his feet and brandishing the paper and the cane to drive Gregor back into his room. Gregor's pleas went unheard; he had not the slightest chance of being understood, no matter how submissively he lowered his head. The more meekly he behaved, the harder his father stamped.'

If you had to choose a scene that encapsulates Franz Kafka's real-life relationship with his own father, it might be this one. Kafka was perfectly open about how incurably bad things remained between them throughout his life. Hermann Kafka was by all accounts a loud, overbearing and impatient blunderbuss. A reasonably prosperous self-made businessman,

Kafka senior was quite unable to understand why his first-born child, Franz, could possibly wish to do other than follow in his footsteps, and help run his ladies' clothing firm. Confronted with a slight, sensitive, artistic and voraciously bookish child, Hermann's reaction was to try to 'toughen him up – knock some sense into the boy'. What on earth was the point of an artist? Instead, the verbal – and perhaps physical – bullying young Franz endured gave rise to the theme that underpins and informs almost all of his work. A weak, innocent and naïve character is forced on a quest to understand, to reason with and, ultimately, to placate an implacable, uncaring force. Since this force is always beyond reason and knowledge, the quest is invariably doomed.

Always the defendant in a trial he can never win, Kafka's anti-hero lives in a kind of quiet, despairing hell, longing only for a peace and reconciliation that are forever denied by a faceless and merciless tyranny. One of his longer novellas is entitled *The Trial [Der Prozess]*, another *The Judgement [Das Urteil]*. It is not surprising, then, that Kafka's work, which seems to have prefigured and even predicted Nazi bestiality, enjoyed a huge resurgence after World War Two.

In *Metamorphosis,* once it becomes clear to the father that his son has become economically useless and a hideous social embarrassment, only the interventions of his mother and sister prevent Herr Samsa from beating him to death. 'He was caught fast and needed help. On one side, his little legs fluttered in the air; on the other they were squashed painfully against the floor. His father struck him a life-threatening blow from behind with the cane. Gregor was sent flying into the bedroom and fell, bleeding heavily. His father slammed the door shut with the stick, and then, at last, all was still.'

Increasingly violent and abusive, later on Gregor's father has another go at murdering him. In a scene of dark comic genius, he sets about Gregor with the contents of the fruit bowl. 'Suddenly something whizzed past him, fell to the ground and rolled away. It was an apple. It was followed immediately by a second one. Paralyzed with terror, Gregor froze.... A weakly thrown apple grazed his back and bounced off harmlessly, but the next one pierced it right through. Gregor's instinct was to drag himself away in the hope that a change of position might alleviate the shocking and unbelievable pain. But he seemed to be nailed fast to the spot and lay spread-eagled, head spinning.'

At the time, Sigmund Freud's theories of subconscious family hatred were being hotly discussed by an enthralled Europe. Kafka acknowledged that a Freudian interpretation of his stories had some value [Freud was a near neighbour in Prague], but insisted it was 'too facile'. He dismissed the value of psychoanalysis in overcoming childhood trauma. To Kafka the whole point of art – or at least his art – was that it stood outside and went beyond simple explanation, into realms of ethical enquiry that made Freud's 'scientific' solutions redundant.

A fan of the Danish theologian Kierkegaard, Kafka was also frank about his interest in the spiritual. Some have interpreted Kafka's work as a commentary on the unknowable divine. In this, much like Kafka's own father, the heavenly father stands eternally apart, all-powerful, unknowable and arbitrary. His workings are so mysterious and beyond the power of

human understanding that, like Abraham ordered to slaughter his first-born son, we can only trust to the good and obey. For Kafka, The Book of Job, with its terrifying and whimsical God, was a defining text.

Not long before he died in 1924, Kafka wrote, 'The reason posterity's appraisal of a man is often more correct than that of his contemporaries is that he is dead. Only after death does a man's true nature emerge. In death, as on the chimney sweep's Saturday night, the soot gets washed from his body. Then it can be seen who did the more harm – his contemporaries to him, or he to his contemporaries. If the latter, he was a great man.'

Wriggling on the pin of sublime ignorance, humanity's attempts to make rational sense of the universe are, in Kafka's scheme of things, absurd. It is a mark of his compassion – and his genius – that he takes the cruel absurdities of life and makes us laugh at them. In so doing he keeps our hope in humanity alive.

William Aaltonen

CHAPTER
I

When Gregor Samsa woke one morning from troubled dreams, he found that he had been transformed – in his bed – into a kind of giant bug. He lay on his back, which had become as hard as armour. Raising his head a little, he saw the arch of a brown abdomen, divided into stiff, domed segments. The quilt was perched precariously on top, and looked as if it might slide off at any moment. A regiment of puny legs, horribly thin compared to the rest of him, quivered wretchedly before his eyes. 'What on earth has happened to me?' he wondered.

It was no dream. His room, which although too small was designed for human occupation, breathed peacefully within its four familiar walls. Above the table, where a collection of cloth samples lay scattered – Samsa was a commercial traveller – hung the picture that he had recently cut from an illustrated magazine and placed in a pretty gilded frame. It showed a lady sitting upright, wearing a fur hat and boa, with her forearm plunged up to the elbow in a heavy fur muff.

Gregor turned his gaze to the window. The dismal weather – raindrops rattled hard on the flashing – made him feel sad. 'What if I just go back to sleep for a bit and forget all this nonsense?' he thought. But with things as they stood that was impossible. He was used to sleeping on his right side, and in his present state there was no way he could adopt that position. The more he tried to force himself over on to his right, the more he kept falling on to his back. He tried a hundred times, closing his eyes so that he did not have to look at his quivering legs, and only gave up when he began to feel a slight, dull ache in his side, of a kind that he had never experienced before.

'God!' he thought. 'What an exhausting job I've chosen. On the road day in and day out – much more stressful than working from home! And apart from the demands of doing business, the actual travelling is so bad: struggling to catch connecting trains, terrible meals at all hours of the day and night, a sea of ever-changing faces and never any chance of making friends. To hell with it all!'

He felt a slight itch at the top of his stomach and slowly hauled himself up to the bedpost on his back, so he could lift his head. There was a scattering of small, white spots at the itchy place, but he had no idea what they meant. He went to explore the area with one of his legs, but drew it back at once – the contact made his blood run cold.

He slid back down into his former position. 'Getting up at the crack of dawn like this,' he said to himself, 'is enough to drive anyone completely insane. A man must have his sleep. The other salesmen live like kept women. When I get back to the hotel in the morning to process my orders, I find these gentlemen still at their breakfast. I'd like to see what my boss would say if I tried that; I'd be out on my ear. Still, that might be a good thing! If I didn't have my parents to think of, I'd have handed in my notice long ago. I'd have gone to the boss and given him a piece of my mind. Knocked him off his perch! Ridiculous, the way he sits up high on his desk, so that he can talk down to us workers from a lofty height – especially when he's so hard of hearing and we all have to stand up close to him! Still, all hope is not lost. Once I've saved the money my parents owe him – which will be in five or six years – I'll definitely go through with it. Take the plunge! In the meantime, I'd better get up: my train goes at five.'

He looked at the alarm clock ticking on the chest. 'Good God!' he thought. It was already half past six, and the minute hand was still creeping steadily forwards – now it was almost a quarter to seven. Had the alarm simply failed? Even from bed he could see the clock was set correctly for four am. It had definitely gone off. Could he really have slept calmly through that earth-shattering din? Calmly, no: his sleep had been anything but peaceful; and yet he had slept perfectly soundly. What exactly, though, was he supposed to do now?

The next train went at seven. To catch it he'd really have to get a move on, and he hadn't even packed his samples yet. The trouble was, he didn't feel in the least bit rested or inclined to get up. Even if he did catch the train, his boss would come down on him hard – the office messenger would have been waiting on the five o'clock train and would long since have told the boss Gregor hadn't turned up. The boy was the manager's creature, a wretched, snivelling toady.

Supposing he called in sick? But that would cause its own problems, and be suspicious, too: during the five years he'd been with the firm he had never once had the slightest illness. The manager would turn up with the Health Insurance doctor. He would reproach his parents for their son's idleness and cut short all objections by repeating the doctor's refrain: there are no sick people in the world, only the workshy. And would he be so far wrong in this case? Apart from the drowsiness that was entirely natural after such a long sleep, Gregor felt in fine form; he was even unusually hungry.

As all these thoughts were racing through his mind, but before he had actually made up his mind to get out of bed, the clock struck quarter to

seven. There was a timid knock on the door by the head of his bed. 'Gregor,' someone called – it was his mother – 'it's quarter to seven. Isn't it time you were on your way?'

What a sweet voice! Gregor trembled as he heard his own in reply. It was unmistakably his voice, but it came with a kind of nasty whining undertone, which meant his words only took proper shape for an instant and then were immediately muffled so that you wondered if you'd really heard them in the first place. Gregor wanted to explain the situation fully; but, given the circumstances, all he said was: 'Yes, yes, thank you, mother – I'm getting up now.' No doubt the door prevented his mother from noticing the change in Gregor's voice, for the explanation reassured her, and she shuffled away in her slippers. Even so, this little exchange had alerted the other members of the family to the fact that Gregor was still in the house. He'd never been this late before. His father started banging on one of the side doors, softly, but with his fists. 'Gregor, Gregor,' he called, 'what's the matter?' And, a moment later, in a louder voice, 'Gregor! Gregor!'

From behind the door on the other side of the room, Gregor's sister called softly, 'Gregor, are you ill? Do you need anything?'

'I'm just coming,' Gregor told them, forcing himself to enunciate carefully and separate each word with a long pause to keep his voice natural. His father went back to breakfast, but his sister kept whispering, 'Gregor, open the door, please!'

Gregor, however, had absolutely no intention of complying; on the contrary, he was pleased he'd got into the habit of always locking the

door on his business trips. He wanted to get up and get dressed without anyone bothering him, and above all, he wanted his breakfast. After that, he'd take time to reflect. There was no way he could make any sensible decisions in bed. He remembered that he often got a mild ache or pain from sleeping awkwardly, which turned out to be imaginary and disappeared as soon as he rose. He was eager to see if this was true of his present condition. As for the change in his voice, he thought privately it must be the sign of a nasty cold, the occupational hazard of travelling salesmen.

He had no difficulty getting rid of the quilt; he only had to puff himself up slightly and it fell clear. But after that, things became much more difficult because his body was now so very much broader. To get up, he needed his arms and hands; but all he had were dozens of little legs, which persisted in wriggling uncontrollably. Before he could bend one leg, he first had to stretch it out; and even when he'd finally managed to make that one behave, all the other little legs kept thrashing about in the most unpleasant and disgusting way. 'I mustn't just lie in bed like a useless lump,' Gregor told himself. To get himself going, he tried to shift the lower part of his body out of bed; but the problem was that this bit of him – which, by the way, he hadn't yet managed to see or even imagine with any clarity – proved too difficult to move.

Slowly beginning to panic, he gathered all his strength and launched himself forward but, getting his aim wrong, he banged hard into one of the bedposts. The searing pain taught him immediately that the lower part of his body was the most sensitive. Next, he tried to manoeuvre the

24

upper part of his new body out of bed. Proceeding with great care, he rotated his head toward the edge of the bed. He managed this quite easily, and the rest of him, despite its mass and size, slowly followed in the same direction. But once his head had cleared the side of the bed and was hanging in mid-air, he was afraid to go any further; if he fell now, it would be a miracle if he didn't crack his skull. This was no time to knock himself unconscious. Better to stay in bed.

But when, panting with fatigue, he found himself stretched out exactly as before, and saw his little legs quivering away more chaotically than ever, he despaired of finding a way of imposing order and peace on all this mess. Again he was forced to the conclusion that he just could not stay in bed, and that if there was the slightest chance of success then the most reasonable course of action was to get up. At the same time, he felt that cool and wise reflection would be far better than rushing into any rash decisions.

At such moments he usually turned his eyes to the window for encouragement and hope. But the fog stopped him from seeing across to the other side of the narrow street, and the view through the glass neither lifted his morale nor gave him confidence. 'Seven o'clock already,' he said as the alarm clock struck the hour for the second time. 'Seven o'clock already, and the fog is still like pea soup!' He lay back again for a while, keeping his breathing shallow – as if, in the complete silence, he could wait calmly for everything, including himself, to return to normal.

Then he said to himself: 'Before it gets to a quarter past, I absolutely have to be up. In any case, they'll send someone from the office, which opens at

seven, to look for me before then.' And he began to rock on his back in an effort to get his whole body out of bed in one go. That way, he would be able to protect his head by snapping it upwards as he fell. His back seemed to be nice and hard; no harm would come to him if he fell on that. His only fear was that the resulting crash, which everyone in the whole house would surely hear, might cause panic, or at the very least make the others anxious. It was a risk he would just have to take.

When Gregor had half his body out of bed – this new way of going at it seemed more like a game than a struggle, since all he had to do was rock himself on his back – he began to think how easily he could have done it if only he had had a little help. Two strong people – his father and the maid came to mind – would have managed it easily. All they would have needed to do was get their arms under his curved back, lift it up from the bed, shift their weight – and his – quickly forward and then simply wait, always taking due care, until he was on the floor where he hoped his feet would at last have found a way of behaving sensibly. But even if the doors had not been closed, would it have been wise for him to call for help? In spite of the desperate circumstances, he couldn't hold back a smile at this thought.

By now he was rocking so far and so hard that he was very close to tipping over, and knew he would have to take a serious decision: in five minutes it would be a quarter to eight. Suddenly there was a knock at the front door. 'Someone from the office,' he thought, and he felt the blood freeze in his veins, while his little legs danced faster than ever. For a moment, all was quiet. 'They're not answering,' Gregor thought with a

wild surge of hope. But then he heard the maid's usual heavy footsteps as she went to the door and opened it. Gregor had only to hear the visitor's first words of greeting to know who it was – the office manager in person. Why was Gregor, of all people, condemned to work for a firm which invariably took the most suspicious view of its employees, and jumped hard on the first sign of any failing? Were all its employees really rogues? Was he the one good and faithful servant among them? Even if he had by chance missed a couple of hours work that morning, he was now so wracked with remorse that he simply couldn't get up.

Couldn't they just have sent one of the trainees to sort things out if they really had to come snooping round? Why did the manager himself have to come, as if to show the whole of Gregor's – entirely blameless – family that only someone of his stature could be trusted to clear up this regrettable affair?

These thoughts annoyed Gregor so much that he swung himself out of bed with a last, almighty heave. It made a loud thud, but not the terrible crash he had feared. The carpet had absorbed some of the impact, and Gregor's back was more flexible than he had imagined, so the noise wasn't too bad. He'd only given his head a bit of a bang. He hadn't kept it high enough, and it had taken a knock in the fall. Cross and in pain, he twisted his head and rubbed it on the carpet.

'Something has just fallen in there,' cried the manager in the room to the left. Gregor tried to imagine the look on his employer's face if *he* had been struck down by a misfortune like this. And why not? As if in brutal reply, the manager began to pace up and down in the next room, which

made his patent leather boots creak. Gregor's sister whispered a warning from the room to the right: 'Gregor, your manager's here.'

'I know,' Gregor muttered, but didn't dare raise his voice enough for her to hear. 'Gregor,' said his father in the room on the left, 'the office manager has come to find out why you didn't catch the early train. We don't know what to say. He wants to speak to you in person. So please open the door. I'm sure he will be kind enough to excuse the untidiness of your room.'

'Good morning, Mr Samsa,' the manager said in a friendly tone.

'He is not well,' his mother said, while his father went on talking through the door. 'Believe me, sir, Gregor is not well. How else could he have missed the train? The boy thinks of nothing but his work! It upsets me to see how he never goes out in the evening. Do you know, he's just spent a whole week in town and he's been at home every night! He sits down with us at the table and stays there, quietly reading the paper or studying his timetables. His greatest relaxation is to do a little fretwork. Why, only the other day he made a small picture frame. He finished it in two or three evenings, and you'd be surprised to see how pretty it is. It's hanging in his room. As soon as Gregor opens his door, you'll be able to see it. I'm so glad you came, sir, as we haven't managed to get Gregor to open his door by ourselves; he is so obstinate. I'm sure he must be ill, even though he says he isn't.'

'I am just coming,' Gregor said slowly and carefully, but he continued to lie still so as not to miss a word of the conversation.

'My dear lady, I can offer no other suggestion,' the manager replied.

'Let us only hope it's nothing serious. But like it or not, we businessmen have to get on with our jobs and ignore our little indispositions.'

'Can the manager come in now?' his father asked impatiently, rapping on the door again.

'No,' Gregor said. There was a painful silence from the room to his left. His sister began to weep in the one on the right. Why didn't she join the others? Perhaps she'd only just got out of bed and wasn't dressed yet. And what was she crying for? Because her brother wouldn't get up to let the manager in? Because he risked losing his job, and because the company director would start pursuing his parents for their outstanding debts again? For the moment, these worries were misplaced. Gregor was still there and hadn't the slightest intention of letting his family down. But at this very moment he was stretched out on the carpet, and nobody seeing him in that state could seriously have asked him to let the manager into his room.

But it was not on account of this slight discourtesy – which in normal circumstances he would easily have found some reason to apologize for later – that Gregor would be dismissed. And he thought it better, for now, to leave the man alone rather than upset him with pleading and tears. But it was exactly his inaction that upset the others and, at the same time, justified their behaviour.

'Mr Samsa,' the manager cried, raising his voice. 'Whatever is the matter? You barricade yourself in your room, you refuse to give us a straight yes or no, you upset your parents needlessly and you neglect your professional duties in the most unheard-of manner. I speak for

your employer and your parents when I demand an immediate explanation.

'I am astonished – astonished! I took you for a quiet, reasonable young man, and here you go suddenly giving yourself airs, behaving in a quite fantastic manner! Speaking to me this morning, the director suggested an explanation for your absence which I rejected – I mean the new sample collection we recently entrusted to your care. I all but gave him my word of honour that this had nothing to do with matters. But now that I have witnessed your stubbornness for myself, Mr Samsa, I can assure you I no longer feel any wish to defend you. Your job is by no means safe. I had intended to tell you this in private but, since you oblige me to waste my time here to no purpose, I see no reason for showing discretion in front of your parents. I'll also have you know that your work has been far from satisfactory of late. We realize, of course, that this time of the year is not the best for business, but you must understand, Mr Samsa, that a period with no business at all cannot, and should not, be tolerated!'

'But, sir,' Gregor cried out to himself, forgetting everything else in his anxiety. 'I will open the door immediately. I will open it. I only felt a little unwell; a slight dizziness stopped me from getting up. I am still in bed. But I feel better already. I am just getting up, really. If you'll only be patient a moment. I am not quite so well as I thought. But I'm all right, really. I don't understand why I've suddenly fallen ill. Only yesterday I felt quite well, as my parents will tell you. And then yesterday evening I felt a bit odd. They must have noticed. Why didn't I tell the office! But

then, you always think you'll be able to shake off an illness without having to stay home. Please spare my parents, sir. The complaints you made just now are really without any foundation. No one has even suggested them before. Perhaps you have not seen the last orders I sent in. I will leave on the eight o'clock train. These few moments of rest have done me the world of good. Please don't waste your time any longer, sir. I shall be at the office immediately. Please tell the director what has happened and put in a good word for me.'

While Gregor was hastily explaining all this, scarcely understanding a word he'd said, he had squirmed up to the wardrobe and begun trying to pull himself upright. His previous gymnastics helped. He wanted to open the door. He wanted to be seen and to speak with the manager. He wanted to know what these people – who kept on harassing him – would say when they saw him. If he frightened them, there would be nothing left to say and they could leave him be. If they took everything calmly, then he had no need to be upset.

If he hurried, he might still be in time to catch the eight o'clock train. The wardrobe was polished, and Gregor slipped several times but, with one final effort, he managed to stand upright. Ignoring the sharp pains in his stomach, he let himself tumble forward on to the top of a nearby chair and clung to it fast with his little legs. Then, finding himself in control of his body, he fell silent so that he could hear what the manager had to say.

'Did you understand a word of what he said?' the manager asked Gregor's parents. 'Is he trying to make fools of us, or what?'

'Merciful God!' Gregor's mother cried, already in tears. 'Perhaps he is seriously ill, and here we are torturing him all this while! Grete! Grete!' she called.

'Mother!' cried her daughter from the other side – they were talking across Gregor's room – 'Fetch a doctor immediately! Gregor is ill! A doctor, quickly! Did you hear him speak?'

'It was an animal's voice,' said the manager. After Mrs Samsa's shrieking, his voice sounded curiously gentle. 'Anna, Anna!' shouted Gregor's father down the hall into the kitchen, clapping his hands. 'Get a locksmith, quick!'

Already the two girls were racing down the hall, skirts rustling – how could his sister have managed to get dressed so quickly? – and tearing out through the front door. Gregor did not hear it close. Perhaps they'd left it open, as so often happens in houses that have suffered disaster.

Gregor felt much calmer. He realized they had not understood his speech, though the words had seemed clear enough to him – clearer, indeed, than before; perhaps because he was getting used to it. But at least they now understood there was something seriously wrong with him, and were ready to help.

The correctness and confident nature of these initial measures made him feel better. He felt as if he were back in the fold of human society, and looked forward to great and wonderful deeds from both the locksmith and the doctor. To clear his throat for the decisive conversation he would soon have to have, he coughed a little, but as quietly as possible, for he feared that even his coughing might not sound human. Meanwhile, in the next room, things had all gone quiet. Perhaps his parents were sitting at the table whispering with the manager; perhaps they were all leaning against the door, listening.

Gregor shuffled slowly towards the door with the chair, threw it aside at the last moment, flung himself at the door and clung upright to the woodwork. The soles of his feet secreted a sticky substance. He rested for a moment. Next, he tried to turn the key in the lock with his mouth. Unfortunately, it seemed he no longer had proper teeth. How could he take hold of the key? On the other hand, he did have a set of very strong jaws. Using these, and ignoring the injury he was probably doing to himself – a brown liquid dribbled from his mouth, trickled over the lock and dripped to the floor – he managed to get hold of the key.

'Listen!' said the manager in the next room. 'He's turning the key.' Gregor took heart at this. He would have liked his father, his mother, everybody to start cheering him on: 'Courage, Gregor, come on, give it all you've got!' Encouraged by the idea that everyone was egging him on, he twisted the key with every last ounce of power his jaws possessed, straining until he nearly passed out. As it turned, he twisted round with it, gripping the key with his mandibles and pressing back up against it with all his weight whenever it slipped. The loud click of the lock as it sprang brought Gregor back to reality. 'They won't need the locksmith now,' he thought, and leaned his head against the handle to open one leaf of the double doors. It was the only way he could have done it, but it prevented the others from actually seeing him, even when the door panel stood almost wide open.

He had to shuffle his way around the edge of the partition with great care, so as not to spoil his entrance by falling flat on his back. He was concentrating on this to the exclusion of everything else when he heard the manager, who was nearest the door, utter a loud 'Oh!'. It sounded like a sudden rush of wind. Gregor saw him clap a hand over his open mouth and slowly stagger back, as if propelled by some invisible and intensely powerful force. His mother, whose hair was still a complete mess despite the manager's presence, shot her husband a look, clasped her hands, took a couple of steps in Gregor's direction and then toppled backward into the arms of her family in a wild confusion of skirts. Her face, which had fallen forward on to her chest, was obscured. Mr Samsa clenched his fists with a menacing air, as if to beat Gregor back into his room; then he cast around the room in bewilderment, covered his eyes with one hand and began weeping so hard the sobs shook his powerful chest.

Gregor stayed out of the room. He stood against the closed half of the double doors, so they could only see a part of his body and, above that, his head, which he now tilted to one side so that he could keep an eye on them. Meanwhile, it had grown much lighter: on either side of the street a part of the long, dark building opposite could clearly be seen – it was a hospital, its grey-black façade pierced by rows of identical, stark windows. It was still raining, in huge drops that smashed to the earth one by one. The breakfast crockery was spread across the table: for his father, breakfast was the most important meal of the day; he would keep it going for hours while he worked his way through various newspapers.

On the wall hung a photograph of Gregor in a lieutenant's uniform, taken while he was in military service; he was smiling, his hand on the hilt of his sword. He looked happy at being respected for his rank. The living-room door was ajar, and, as the front door was also open, there was a clear view out to the landing and the top of the stairs.

'Now,' Gregor said – he realized he was the only one to have kept calm – 'now I will get dressed, pack my samples, and go. Will you please let me go? Surely you can see now, sir, that I am not just being difficult and that I fully intend to work. Commercial travelling is tiresome, and no mistake, but without it I cannot live. Where are you going, sir? To the office? Yes? Will you tell them the truth about everything? Everybody has a day off now and again, and that's the time to review their work record: once things improve, they go back to the grindstone and work better than ever. I owe the director a great deal, as you know. And I have my parents and my sister to think about. I'm in an awkward position, but I shall return to work. Only, please do not make things more difficult for me – they're hard enough as it is. Speak up for me at the office. I know they don't like the salesmen. They think we earn too much money, and lead an easy life.

'The present situation doesn't exactly help overcome this prejudice; but you, sir, as manager, can judge the circumstances better than the rest of the staff, better than the director himself –– between ourselves, as the boss he is often misled by unfair talk. You know quite well that the travelling salesman, who barely sets foot in the office from one year to the next, is often the victim of gossip, or of random sniping against which

he is powerless to defend himself for the simple reason that he usually doesn't even know what he is being accused of. He only learns about it when he comes home exhausted at the end of a trip, or when the unfortunate consequences of some business he can no longer even remember return to haunt him. Don't leave without a word or two to show that you give me some credit.'

But as soon as Gregor started to speak the manager turned away, only glancing back with a twitch of his shoulder and pursed lips. He had not been idle while Gregor was speaking; instead, he had retreated furtively, step by step, towards the door – making sure he kept a close eye on Gregor at all times – sneaking off as if there were some unwritten law against leaving the room. Already he had reached the hall. He took his last steps out of the living-room as if the soles of his shoes were on fire. As he exited, he stretched his right hand out blindly towards the stairs as if some divine deliverance awaited him below.

Gregor realized that if he let the manager go as things stood, then he could probably kiss goodbye to his job. Unfortunately, his parents did not share in his moment of clarity; they'd long believed that Gregor was settled in the firm for life and were so consumed by their present grief that they had no idea what to make of it all. But Gregor was thinking ahead. The manager had to be stopped, calmed, convinced and finally won over. His own and his family's future depended on it!

If only his sister were there! She had understood; she had actually begun to cry while Gregor was still lying quietly on his back. The manager, who was a ladies' man, would have listened to her, let her guide him. She

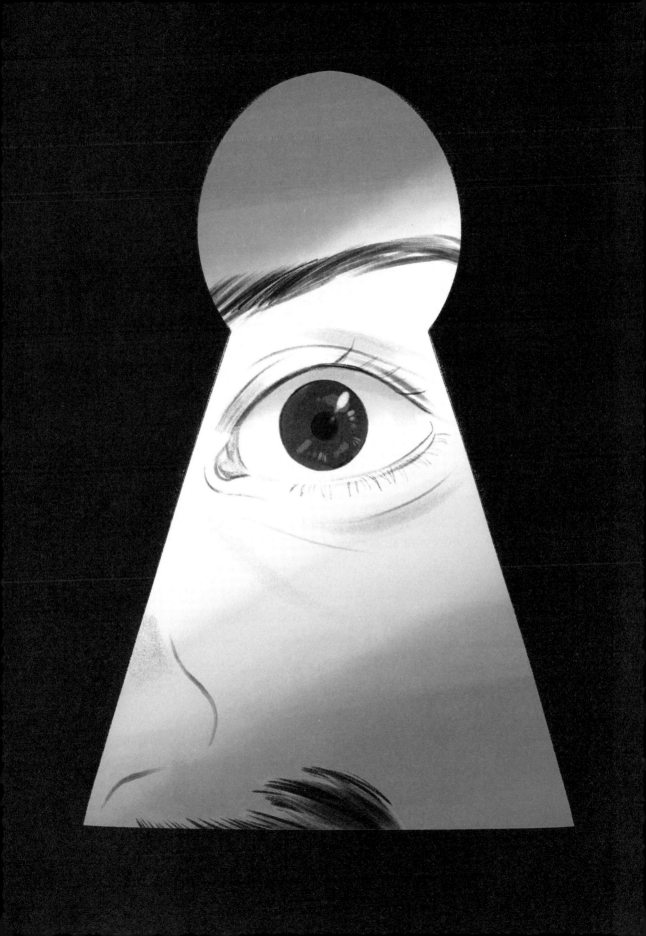

would have closed the living-room door and convinced him, out there on the landing, that his terror was unfounded. But there was no sign of her. Gregor would just have to deal with the problem himself. And without even stopping to wonder whether he was physically up to the task, or whether his little speech had even been understood, he let go of the partition, shoved himself out through the door in an effort to overtake the manager (by now he was clinging to the banisters with both hands in the most ridiculous manner), made a vain attempt to catch himself and then, with a sharp cry, fell forward on to his scurrying feet.

Suddenly, and for the first time that morning, he experienced a feeling of physical wellbeing. Not only were his feet now on firm ground, but he noticed with a pang of joy that his legs obeyed him wonderfully; they were eager to carry him wherever he wanted. Maybe his troubles were all behind him now. He scuttled up to his mother and began rocking back and forth. At this point he saw her suddenly snap out of her faint, jump up, throw her arms in the air and shout, 'Help! For God's sake, help!' She tilted her head to get a better look at Gregor. Then, as if thinking better of it, she began careering backwards, completely forgetting that the table, still covered with all the breakfast things, was directly behind her. She staggered right into it and sat down almost absent-mindedly, hardly noticing that the overturned coffee pot right next to her was belching its contents all over the carpet.

'Mother, mother,' Gregor said quietly, looking up at her. He had quite forgotten about the manager. Seeing the coffee spilling, without thinking Gregor found himself snapping his mandibles in the air.

At this, his mother started shrieking again, jumped up from the table and fell into the arms of her husband, who had rushed up behind her. But Gregor had no time to worry about them. The manager was already on the stairs; resting his chin on the banister, he was looking back for one last time.

Gregor sprang forward to try and stop him. The manager must have guessed what was coming, for he leapt down the steps in a single bound and vanished with a cry of 'Aaagh!' which echoed through the stairwell. His rapid escape had the unfortunate effect of causing Gregor's father – who until now had kept a hold of himself – to fly completely off the handle. Instead of running after the manager, or at least not trying to stop Gregor from overhauling him, he seized the manager's walking stick in his right hand – he had left it behind on a chair, along with his overcoat and hat – grabbed a large newspaper from the table to his left and began stamping his feet and brandishing the paper and the cane to drive Gregor back into his room. Gregor's pleas went unheard; he had not the slightest chance of being understood no matter how submissively he lowered his head. The more meekly he behaved, the harder his father stamped.

Across from them, and despite the cold, Mrs Samsa had thrown the window open and was leaning out as far as possible, her face pressed into her hands. A great draught of air swept up the stairs from the street. The curtains billowed, the papers blew up and a few sheets flew across the room. Hissing savagely, Gregor's father came after him. Unused to moving backwards, Gregor beat a slow retreat. If only he'd been able to turn around he'd have reached his room in no time. But he was afraid

that if the treacle slowness of his retreat made his father any more impatient, then his reward would be a lethal blow from the stick to the head or back.

Gregor quickly ran out of options. To his horror, he realized that he had no control when he was in reverse gear. Watching his parent fearfully out of the corner of his eye, he tried his hardest to speed up the turn. It was taking forever. Perhaps his father realized he meant well: instead of hindering him, he was now helping shove Gregor round with the tip of the stick. If only he would stop that unbearable hissing! It was driving Gregor mad. He had almost completed his turn when, confused by all the din, he lost his sense of direction and began lumbering back round to face his father. He was just celebrating the fact that he'd got his head through the half-opened double doors, when he discovered that without even more of a performance his body was too wide to go through them.

Naturally, in his present mood it never occurred to his father to open the other side of the door so that Gregor could pass through. The one idea in his head was to get the boy back into his room as quickly as possible.

His father didn't have the patience to wait for Gregor to haul himself upright and get into his room that way. Right on his heels and making enough noise for a hundred fathers, not one, his father badgered Gregor to get through the door as if that was the easiest thing in the world. This wasn't funny any more. Throwing caution to the winds, Gregor hurled himself at the gap. One side of his body stuck fast in the doorway, lacerated

by the door jamb, whose white paint was now covered in horrible brown stains. He was caught fast and needed help.

On one side, his little legs fluttered helplessly in the air; on the other they were squashed painfully against the floor. His father struck him a life-threatening blow from behind with the cane. Gregor was sent flying into the bedroom and fell, bleeding heavily. His father slammed the door shut with the stick, and then, at last, all was still.

CHAPTER
2

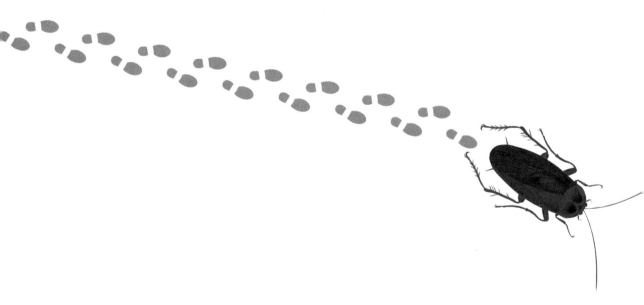

It was dusk by the time Gregor woke from his heavy, swoon-like sleep. He would have woken up anyway even without any disturbance – he felt fully rested – but it seemed to him that he'd been spooked by the furtive rattle of a key in the lock of the hall door.

Here and there, the ceiling and furniture caught the muted play of light reflected from the electric tramway. But down where Gregor lay all was dark. He hauled himself slowly towards the door in an effort to work out what had happened, probing clumsily with the feelers which he was only now beginning to master. His left side seemed to him to be one long, painful scar, and he was limping on his double set of legs. One leg had been seriously injured in the course of the morning's events – it was a miracle more of them hadn't been damaged – and it dragged lifelessly behind him.

When he reached the door, he realized what had attracted him: the smell of food. There was a bowl of sweetened milk there, with little pieces of bread floating in it. He could have chuckled with delight; he was even hungrier than he had been in the morning. He plunged his head in the milk up to his eyes. Immediately, he withdrew it; his tender left side made eating difficult, and in fact he could only manage by contorting his whole body and snorting. But the thing was, he could no longer bear the smell of milk which had once been his favourite drink and which his sister had no doubt brought specially. He turned away from the bowl in disgust and dragged himself to the middle of the room.

The gas was lit in the living-room – he could see it through the cracks in the door. Under normal circumstances, this was the time of day when his father entertained the family by reading aloud from the evening paper; but for the moment all was quiet. Perhaps this ritual, which his sister always told him about in her letters, had recently died out. Everything was silent, and yet surely there had to be someone in the room? 'What a quiet life my family has led,' thought Gregor, staring into the darkness, and he felt very proud that he was the one who had provided his parents and his sister with their tranquil life and their lovely flat.

What would happen now, if this peace, this happiness, this wellbeing were to end in terror and disaster? To push away these gloomy thoughts, Gregor began to take a little exercise, crawling backwards and forwards across the floor.

At one point during the evening he saw the door on the left open slightly, and another time it was the door on the right: someone seemed to think about coming in, but decided not to risk it. Gregor waited by the dining-room door, willing on the hesitant visitor as best he might, or at least hoping to see who it was; but it never opened again, and Gregor stood sentry in vain. That morning, when the door had been locked, everyone had tried to invade his room; but now that they had managed to open it, no one came to see him. They had even locked the doors on the outside.

The lights in the living-room stayed on until late, and Gregor knew his parents and sister were still up; he heard the three of them stealing away on tiptoe. That meant no one would come and see him before morning, which gave him plenty of time to think about how he was going to manage his new life. But now that he had to keep his stomach

down flat to the floor, the enormous room he had lived in for the past five years frightened him in a way he could not comprehend.

Half-heartedly and somewhat ashamed, he fled under the sofa, where he soon found that he felt more comfortable, even though his back was slightly squashed and he could not raise his head fully. He was only sorry his body was too thick to fit right under it. He spent the whole night there in a half-sleep, broken by sharp pangs of hunger and vague hopes and worries. These led him to conclude that it was his duty to remain quiet and patient at all costs, and to try to make things as bearable as he could for his family, despite the unpleasant turn of events.

Early in the morning he had a chance to test the strength of his new resolution. It was only just growing light. His sister, who was already almost fully dressed, opened the hall door and looked in curiously. At first, she didn't see him, and must have thought, 'He must be somewhere, for heaven's sake, he can't just have flown away.' Then, when she spotted him under the sofa, she was so scared she rushed back out again, slamming the door behind her. A moment later, regretting her behaviour, she opened it for the second time and tiptoed in, as if entering the room of a stranger or someone who was seriously ill.

Gregor stuck his head out from the side of the sofa and watched her. Would she notice that he'd left the milk, and realize it was not because he wasn't hungry? Would she bring him some other food that suited him better? If she didn't do so of her own accord, he would rather have starved to death than draw her attention to it, despite his tremendous urge to

shoot forward out of his hiding place, throw himself at his sister's feet and beg her for something nice to eat.

In fact his sister noticed the brimming bowl immediately. Her eyes widened. Some milk had spilled around it; using a piece of paper, of course, and not her bare hands, she picked the bowl up and carried it off to the kitchen. Gregor was extremely curious to see what she would bring him instead, and all kinds of things came into his mind. But he would never have guessed what his sister, in her kindness, actually did. To find out what her brother really liked to eat, she brought a whole range of options spread out on an old newspaper. There were half-rotten chunks of vegetables; bones from the family supper covered in congealed white sauce; a few currants and raisins; some almonds; some cheese that Gregor had recently decided was inedible; a stale loaf; a piece of salted bread and butter, and another slice of bread without the salt. She also set down the bowl again, the one which was almost certainly now earmarked for Gregor's exclusive use and which she had filled with water. Showing great consideration in understanding that her brother would prefer not to eat in front of her, she then left, closing and locking the door so that he could eat in peace and quiet.

As he headed for the food, Gregor felt all his little legs start to tremble beneath him. His wounds seemed to have healed, for he moved with complete freedom, which amazed him when he remembered that he'd cut his finger more than a month earlier, and that it had still been hurting as recently as two days before.

'Am I less vulnerable now?' he wondered. But he had already started

sucking eagerly at the cheese, for which he had developed a singular and sudden craving. In quick succession, he devoured the cheese, the vegetables and the sauce, tears of pure joy streaming from his eyes. But he wouldn't go near the fresh food – the smell of it repelled him, and he pushed it further away so that it wouldn't put him off the rest.

Long after he'd finished, he was drowsing idly in the same spot when his sister turned the key in the lock, softly and slowly so that he'd have time to hide. Even though he was still half asleep, he got the wind up and hurried back to the sofa. It took all his self-control to stay under it for the short time his sister was in the room: the heavy meal had made him a bit fatter, so that he could scarcely breathe in the tight space. Struggling for breath, he watched tearfully as his sister, assuming he no longer wanted it, swept up the remains of his meal and the things that he hadn't touched, dropped the trash into a bucket, covered it with a wooden lid and took it away. Almost before she'd turned her back, Gregor struggled out from his hiding place, stretched and let his body expand to its proper size.

That's how he was fed every day. In the morning, before his parents and the maid were awake, and in the afternoon, when lunch was over and while his parents were taking a short nap – and his sister had given the maid a task to keep her busy. They certainly didn't want Gregor to die of hunger, but they probably didn't choose to know any more about how he ate his food than they were told. Perhaps, too, Gregor's sister wanted to spare them any more heartache than they were no doubt already enduring.

Gregor never learned what excuses they had made to get the doctor and the locksmith out of the apartment, because while he could understand what other people said, no one, not even his sister, imagined that he could do so. When she came into his room, he had to content himself with listening to her sighing and invoking the saints. It was only much later, when they had become a bit more used to the changed situation – obviously, they were never going to get used to it entirely – that Gregor would occasionally overhear a few words betraying what seemed to him like kindness. When he had eaten all the food off the newspaper she would say, 'He liked what I brought today.' At other times, when he had no appetite – and as time went on this became more frequent – she would tell them with a certain sadness, 'He didn't touch a thing today.'

Even if he couldn't get any direct news, Gregor overheard a good deal of what was said in the dining-room. As soon as he picked up the sound of voices, he would hurry to the appropriate door and press the length of his body tight up against it. In the early days, especially, there was little conversation, secret or otherwise, that did not bear more or less directly on his predicament. For two whole days, mealtimes were given over to discussions about the best way to handle things. Even between meals, the talk was mainly the same. At least two members of the family were always at home – none of them wanted to be there alone, but under no circumstances could they leave the apartment unattended.

It was not entirely clear how much the cook knew, but, on the very first day, she had fallen on her knees and begged Mrs Samsa to let her go at once. A quarter of an hour later, she thanked them tearfully on

her way out, as if letting her quit was the greatest, kindest thing they had ever done for her. And without being asked to do so, she swore a terrible oath never to reveal even the slightest hint about what she knew to anyone.

Now Gregor's mother and sister had to do the cooking, but this wasn't too troublesome since no one was eating very much. Occasionally Gregor would hear one of them vainly exhorting another to eat. The reply was always more or less the same: 'I'm full, thanks.' They didn't really drink much, either. Often his sister would ask her father if he'd like some beer. She'd offer to fetch it, or, faced with his silence and to get round him, she'd suggest that the janitor's wife go for it. But each time her father replied with a loud 'No!' and that was the end of it.

On day one of the crisis, Mr Samsa had given his wife and daughter a clear account of their financial situation and future prospects. From time to time, he would get up from the table and hunt for some document or account book in his small Wertheim safe, which he'd rescued from the failure of his business five years earlier. They all heard him opening and closing the complicated locks, taking things out and relocking it. His father's announcement was the most heartening thing Gregor had heard since becoming a prisoner. He had always imagined that his father had been unable to save a penny from the ruins of his business. That's because his father had never said anything to the contrary, and Gregor had never asked. His only concern had been to do everything he could to help his family forget the financial disaster that had plunged them all into such despair as quickly as possible.

He had set to work with exemplary enthusiasm; almost overnight he had been promoted from junior clerk to commercial traveller, with all the benefits the new job entailed – not least the prospect of earning more money. And in very short order, his efforts were transformed into ready money, laid out on the table before his family's surprised and delighted eyes. Happy days, never since recaptured, even though later on Gregor had made so much money that he'd been able to shoulder the family's entire financial burden.

His family had grown to accept this state of affairs as much as Gregor. He gave the money willingly, they took it gratefully, but the arrangement no longer gave rise to any special warmth. Only his sister had kept a place in her heart for Gregor, who planned to pay for her to enter the Conservatory the following year, regardless of the high fees which he would just have to find some other way. Unlike Gregor, his sister was very fond of music and wanted to study the violin, which she played with some skill. The Conservatory often came up in the fleeting conversations they had when Gregor snatched a few hours at home, but almost always in the guise of happy daydreaming. Their parents didn't much like even these innocent reveries, but Gregor took the matter very seriously, and had set his heart on announcing the plan officially come Christmas Eve.

Even though they were pointless in his present situation, it was ideas like this that teemed in Gregor's thoughts when he was pressed up against the door listening. Sometimes, he grew so tired he could listen no more, and his head would accidentally bump against the panelling; but he

would snatch it back at once, since they'd notice even the slightest noise in the room beyond and fall silent.

'What on earth is he up to now?' his father would say after a pause, no doubt with a nod at the door; and only then did they pick up the interrupted conversation. Since his father was often obliged to repeat his explanation in order to recall details he himself had long forgotten, or to make his wife understand – she did not always grasp things the first time around – Gregor discovered that, despite all their misfortunes, his parents had been able to save a small sum of money, and that the untouched interest on this had meantime helped it grow.

Neither had they spent all of the monthly wages that Gregor, keeping only a couple of shillings for himself, had handed over every week. This had enabled them to accumulate a little more capital. Behind the door, Gregor nodded approvingly, delighted at this unexpected foresight and thrift. It was true that his father could have paid off his debt to Gregor's employer with these savings much sooner, and so brought Gregor's release date nearer; but under the circumstances it was much better that his father had acted as he had.

Unfortunately, the interest on the capital wasn't enough for the family to live on: it would last a year, perhaps two, but no longer. That nest egg had to be kept for emergencies. They would have to earn the money to pay the bills.

Despite his good health, Mr Samsa was nonetheless an old man who hadn't worked for five years – no one could really expect too much of him. During these five years of retirement – his first holiday in a life

dedicated to hard work and failure – he had become extremely fat and slow-moving. And suffering as she did from asthma, old Mrs Samsa wouldn't be able to earn much, either. In fact, nowadays, just getting around the house was an effort, and she spent every other day lying on the sofa, wheezing for breath by the open window. Was his sister – a child, still, at 17 – supposed to become the breadwinner? Her life so far – she was always nicely dressed and rested, helping a little about the house, enjoying a few modest amusements and above all devoted to her violin – had not prepared her for anything so taxing. Whenever the conversation turned to the subject of earning money, Gregor would leave his post by the door and fall back on to the nearby sofa, whose cool leather was so soothing to his body, burning as it was with anxiety and shame.

Often he lay sleepless the whole night, scratching at the leather for hours on end. At other times, he would eagerly push his armchair over to the window, pull himself up on the casement, wedge himself against the seat and lean forward against the panes; not so much to savour the view as to re-live the happiness he'd felt there before. In reality, he could now barely make out the hospital – whose unremitting bulk he had once cursed – directly opposite. If he hadn't been certain he lived in the quiet but entirely urban confines of Charlottenstrasse, he might well have believed his window looked out on to a wasteland, where the grey of the sky and the grey of the earth merged indistinguishably. His attentive sister had only to see the armchair by the window twice to understand; from then on, each time she tidied the room she would push the armchair up to the window, and leave the lower half of the casement open.

If only Gregor had been able to speak to her and thank her for doing so much for him, he could have accepted her services more easily. As it was, they both pained and embarrassed him. Naturally she tried to pass things off as lightly as possible, and as time went on she played her part even better; but she could not prevent her brother from understanding with increasing clarity how matters stood.

He began to dread her visits. The moment she came into the room – hurriedly shutting the door as if she wanted to spare the others the sight of what lay within – she would run to the window, fling it open and stick her head out, breathing deeply for a minute no matter how cold it was, as if to prevent imminent suffocation. Twice a day, while he lay trembling under the sofa, she terrified Gregor with all this rush and clatter. He knew his sister would have spared him this ordeal if she'd been able to stand being in the same room with him with the window shut.

One day – it must have been a good month after Gregor's metamorphosis, and his sister could hardly have had any reason to be surprised at his appearance – she came a little earlier than usual and found him looking out of the window. He was motionless, but something in the way he was standing struck fear into her heart. Gregor wouldn't have been surprised if she'd stayed out of the room – his position prevented her from opening the window. But not only would she not enter, she sprang back, slammed the door and locked it.

A stranger might have thought that Gregor was planning to bite her. Of course, Gregor hid under the sofa at once, but it was noon before his sister ventured back and, when she did turn up, she looked much more

agitated than usual. From this, he deduced that his appearance still disgusted her, that it always would and that it was only by exercising the most terrific self-control that she stopped herself running from the room the moment she caught sight of the tiniest part of his body protruding from under the sofa. To spare her the awful sight, one day Gregor took a sheet on his back, dragged it to the sofa – it took him four hours – and arranged it in such a way that his sister couldn't see him even if she bent down. If she hadn't wanted this screen, then she could have removed it – it was clear he wasn't hiding for fun.

But his sister left the sheet where it was, and Gregor, prudently parting the fabric with his head to see how she was taking the new arrangement, thought he detected a look of gratitude on her face. During the first fortnight his parents had not been able to bring themselves to enter his room. He often heard them praising his sister's hard work, whereas before they had frequently complained that she was a useless young girl. But now, both his father and mother would often wait outside Gregor's door while she was tidying the room, and scarcely had she come out again than they would make her tell them in detail exactly how she had found things in there: what had Gregor eaten, exactly what was he doing and was there any sign of improvement, however slight? His mother had wanted to see Gregor almost from the first, but his father and sister had dissuaded her with sensible arguments, to which Gregor listened very attentively and with which he wholly agreed.

Later, however, they had to hold her back by force, and when his mother began to cry, 'Let me go to Gregor! My poor boy! Don't you understand that I have to see him!' Gregor thought that perhaps it might be a good thing after all if his mother came in, not every day, of course, but perhaps once a week: she would understand things better than his sister, who for all her courage was still only a child, and had in all likelihood only taken on such a difficult job out of naïve goodwill.

Gregor's hopes of seeing his mother were soon fulfilled. He avoided showing himself at the window during the day out of consideration for his parents; but he couldn't crawl very far on the few square metres of his bedroom floor, and found it hard to lie quietly at night. Since he no longer enjoyed eating, he took to scuttling around the room to distract himself: up and down the walls and across the ceiling, from which he liked to hang upside down. It was much better than crawling across the floor – he breathed more easily, his body vibrated with pleasure, and he sometimes lost himself so completely in the moment that much to his surprise he'd let go and come crashing down. But now that he had better control over his body, he managed to make these headlong plunges harmless.

His sister immediately noticed the new pastime Gregor had devised for himself – even at a crawl he left a trail of sticky marks everywhere – and took it into her head to help him beetle about as freely as possible by removing all the furniture that might get in his way, especially the wardrobe and the writing desk. Unfortunately, she was not strong enough to manage this on her own and didn't dare ask her father to lend a hand. As for the sixteen-year-old maid, there was no way she'd have agreed to help – the child had worked with a will since the former cook had been let go, but only on condition that she could keep the kitchen door locked,

and open it only when specially requested. So his sister would just have to ask her mother to help one day when her father was out. Mrs Samsa consented gladly, but her loud cries of pleasure ceased abruptly when she reached Gregor's door.

Of course, his sister made sure everything in the room was in order first; then she allowed her mother to go in. In his extreme haste, Gregor had pulled the sheet down further than usual, and the folds made it look as if it had just been thrown over the sofa by chance. This first time, he stopped himself from peeping out under the sheet to see his mother, but he was delighted to have her nearby. 'Come in – you can't see him,' his sister said, and obviously taking her mother by the hand, she led her into the room. Then Gregor heard the two frail women struggling to move the heavy old wardrobe. His sister did most of the work, despite her mother's warnings that she might overstrain herself. It took a very long time.

They had been struggling with the monster wardrobe for about a quarter of an hour when Mrs Samsa declared it might be best to leave the thing where it was: in the first place, it was too heavy for them, and they wouldn't be able to finish moving it before Mr Samsa came back. Secondly, if they left the wardrobe in the middle of the room, then Gregor might find it got in his way. Finally, who knew whether or not he'd be pleased if they moved his furniture out? Mrs Samsa thought he wouldn't; the sight of the bare walls made her heart ache. How could Gregor not feel the same, when he'd lived with all this furniture for so long; how could he possibly not feel abandoned in a bare room? 'In any case,' she said in a low voice – she had spoken in whispers ever since she came in, not so much because Gregor, whose lair she had not yet discovered, might hear her words – she was convinced he couldn't understand these – but so he would not have to listen to the sound of her voice. 'In any case, if we move all the stuff out, aren't we more or less saying we've given up all hope of seeing him cured? Are we just going to leave him to his fate? I think it would be better to keep everything just as it was, so that when Gregor comes back to us he'll find everything the same – and it will be easier for him to forget what's happened.'

Hearing his mother's words, Gregor realized that the monotonous life he'd been leading for the past two months, in the course of which no one had spoken a single word to him, must have turned his mind. He could not otherwise explain his overwhelming desire for a nice empty room. Did he really want this warm, comfortable den filled with all the family furniture to be transformed into an empty cave, where he could crawl about to his heart's content – and wave a swift goodbye to his human past? Had he come so close to forgetting it already? It had taken nothing less than his mother's voice, which he hadn't heard for so long, to wake him up. Nothing should be removed; everything had to remain as it was. The furniture had to stay because it was keeping him sane; if it prevented him from utterly losing his wits and crawling aimlessly around the place, then so much the better.

Unfortunately, his sister had other plans. She'd grown used to taking charge of her parents when it came to Gregor. There was good reason for all this, and now her mother's remarks were enough to make her decide

to remove not only the writing desk and the wardrobe – which up till then had been her sole aim – but all of the other furniture as well, except of course for the indispensable sofa. This wasn't just out of childish contrariness, nor just because of the hard-won and recent self-confidence she had so unexpectedly acquired. No, she really believed that Gregor needed plenty of room to run about in, and that, as far as she could tell, he never used the furniture.

Perhaps, also, the passionate nature of girls her age played a part – her way was to seek out every opportunity for self-expression, and it now drove her to make her brother's life even more difficult, as she strove to do more and more on his behalf.

Only Grete dared enter and stay in the room over whose bare walls Gregor reigned supreme. She ignored her mother, who seemed ill-at-ease in there, and who now fell silent, doing her best to help move the wardrobe. Gregor could just about put up with that going, but the desk had to stay. And hardly had the women left the room, panting as they pushed the wardrobe, than Gregor stuck his head out from under the sofa to see if he might make a prudent and tactful intervention. But unfortunately it was his mother who returned first. Grete was next door, arms around the wardrobe, pulling and pushing it, but unable to get it into place.

Gregor knew his mother wasn't used to the sight of him; he didn't want her to pass out with fright. Terrified, he reversed hurriedly towards the other end of the sofa, but in doing so inadvertently knocked the sheet. His mother couldn't help but notice. She stopped short, stood stock still for a moment and then hurried back to Grete. Although Gregor kept

telling himself that nothing out of the ordinary was happening – that they were just moving a few pieces of furniture – there was no doubt that the commotion the women were making, their muted cries, the scraping of the furniture, was unnerving him. However much he kept his head down, drew his legs up and pressed himself flat, he knew he couldn't bear all of this for much longer. They were emptying his room, taking everything he loved; they had already taken the wardrobe, where he kept his saw and his fretwork kit; now they were shifting his desk, which had stood so solidly in place all these years, the very same desk where he'd done his homework when he was in business college, at secondary school and even back in primary school.

He really didn't have any time left to worry about the good intentions of these two women. In any case he'd almost forgotten their existence: by now they were so tired they were working almost in silence, and the only sound he could hear was the thumping of their feet. So Gregor came out of his lair. The women were leaning against the desk in the next room taking a short breather – and he found himself so bewildered that he changed direction four times. He couldn't make up his mind what to try and save first; then he suddenly caught sight of his picture of the woman dressed in furs, stark on the bare wall. He scuttled up and pressed himself against the glass, which felt good stuck fast to his hot belly. At least no one could take the picture now that he was spread-eagled all over it. He turned his head toward the living-room door to watch them coming back.

They'd only taken a short break and now here they were. Grete had

her arm round her mother and was almost dragging her along. 'Well, what shall we do next?' Grete said, looking around. Her gaze met Gregor's as he hung on the wall. It was probably only out of concern for her mother that she kept any composure. She leaned her head forward to stop her mother from seeing anything and said a little too quickly and in a trembling voice, 'Come on, let's go back to the living-room for a minute.'

Grete's eyes told Gregor what she had in mind: she was going to get her mother to safety and then come back and chase him down off the wall. Well, let her try! He lay over his picture, determined not to give it up. He would sooner leap into his sister's face. But Grete's words had served to upset her mother; at that very moment, Mrs Samsa turned, saw the gigantic brown blob on the wallpaper and, before she had time to take in the fact it was her son, screamed, 'O God! O God!' and fell back on to the sofa and lay motionless, arms flung wide in total horror.

'You – Gregor!' Grete cried, raising her fist and shooting him a withering look. They were the first words she'd spoken to him directly since his transformation. She ran through to the next room, to fetch something to revive her mother. Gregor decided to help – there was still time to save the picture – but found he was stuck fast to the glass and had to make a violent effort to break free. He hurried after his sister, meaning to give her more of the same good advice he'd handed out in the past. But he could only stand and watch as she rummaged among the bottles. Then he frightened her so terribly when she turned round that a bottle fell and shattered on the floor. A splinter from this wounded

Gregor in the face, and he found himself covered in some kind of corrosive medicine. Grete snatched up as many bottles as she could carry and rushed in to her mother, slamming the door behind her with her foot.

Now there was no way Gregor could reach his mother, and it was his fault if she was at death's door. He didn't dare go and look in case he drove his sister away again; she had to stay with his mother. There was nothing he could do but wait. Gnawed by self-reproach and anxiety, he began crawling all over the place: across the walls, the furniture, the ceiling, until finally, in a torment of despair and, as his head began to spin, he fell heavily, slap bang on to the middle of the big table.

Some time passed while Gregor lay dazed where he'd fallen. Everything was quiet. Perhaps that was a good sign. Then the bell rang. With the maid barricaded in the kitchen as usual, Grete had to go and open the front door. His father was back. The first thing he said was, 'What happened?' Grete's expression told him everything he needed to know. In a stifled voice – she probably had her face buried in her father's chest – she said, 'Mother fainted, but she's much better now. Gregor has escaped.'

'Just what I expected,' her father replied. 'I told you all along, but you women will never listen.'

It was clear to Gregor that his father had misunderstood Grete's all too brief explanation and imagined that his son was guilty of some violent act. Since there was no time and no possibility of making him understand, he had to find some way of pacifying his father. He rushed to the bedroom door and pressed himself up against it, so that when he came in from the hallway his father would know he meant to go back into his own room

immediately, and there was no need to drive him back by force. All he needed to do was open the door, and Gregor would shoot back inside.

But his father was in no mood for niceties. As he entered he cried, 'Ha!' in a tone that suggested he was both furious and pleased at the same time. Gregor drew his head back from the door and turned to look at his father. He was amazed. He had never imagined his father could look as he now did. It was true that Gregor had been so taken up with the lovely new sensation of crawling around that he hadn't really kept up with what was going on in the house, and had therefore not become aware of certain changes. And yet – and yet, was that really his father? Was this really the same man who once had lain buried wearily in bed when Gregor was setting off on his business trips? Who met him, on his return, still in his dressing gown, wedged into an armchair from which he couldn't even lift himself, or do any more than raise his arms to show how pleased he was? Was this that same old man who, on the rare walks they took together as a family, two or three Sundays a year and on special holidays, would hobble ever more slowly between Gregor and his mother – who in any case walked slowly enough – bundled up in an old coat, probing cautiously ahead with his walking stick as he struggled to make progress? And who, when he wanted to say something, would stop dead and gather his family around him?

Now here he was, a fine, upstanding citizen, dressed in a tight-fitting blue uniform with gold buttons of the kind worn by bank employees. His monumental double chin spread its imposing folds above a high, stiff collar; dark, watchful eyes peered keenly out from beneath the bushy eyebrows;

normally untidy, his white hair now featured a painfully exact parting. He threw his cap, which seemed to be decorated with the gold monogram of some bank, in a neat arc across the room on to the sofa. Then, with his hands in his trouser pockets, the long tails of his coat turned back, he walked toward Gregor with a menacing air.

In fact, he was probably unsure about what he was going to do; but he lifted his feet quite immoderately high in the air. Gregor was astonished at the enormous size of his father's boot soles. But he had no time to dwell on that. From the very first day of his new life he'd known that his father believed he should be treated with the utmost severity. And so he scuttled ahead of him, stopping whenever he stopped and scurrying off again at his father's slightest movement. They circled the room several times in this way without matters coming to a head. Truth be told, their movements were so slow it didn't even look like a proper chase. Gregor stayed on the floor, not least because he was afraid that if his father saw him climbing about the walls or rushing across the ceiling he'd take it as a sign of particular malice. And yet, he knew things couldn't go on like this for very much longer.

In the short time it took his father to take one step, Gregor had to make a whole series of rippling gymnastic movements, and as he'd never had good lungs, he was already growing noticeably short of breath. He staggered along, concentrating all his strength on running away, scarcely able to keep his eyes open, so dazed that all he could think of was escape. He had almost forgotten that he could use the walls, although in this room all the finely carved furniture, with its serrations and sharp points,

worked against him. Suddenly something whizzed past him, fell to the ground and rolled away. It was an apple. It was followed immediately by a second one.

Paralyzed with terror, Gregor froze. It was no good trying to run any more – his father had decided to bombard him. He had filled his pockets with the contents of the fruit bowl on the sideboard, and was flinging one apple after another, without – at least for the moment – even taking proper aim. The little red apples rolled about the floor, colliding with one another as if electrified. A weakly thrown apple grazed his back and bounced off harmlessly, but the next one pierced it right through. Gregor's instinct was to drag himself away in the hope that a change of position might alleviate the shocking and unbelievable pain. But he seemed to be nailed fast to the spot and lay spread-eagled, head spinning. With his last glance, he saw his bedroom door suddenly flung wide, and his mother dash out in front of his sister who was shouting at the top of her voice.

His mother was in her undergarments: to ease the grip of her fainting fit his sister had partly undressed her so that she could breathe more easily. Then he saw his mother run to his father, her untied petticoats slipping to the floor one after another. Tripping over her skirts, she fell forward against her husband, put her arms around him, hugged him tight and, clasping the back of his neck – at which point Gregor's eyesight failed him – begged him to spare Gregor's life.

CHAPTER
3

The apple which no one dared remove from Gregor's back remained embedded in his flesh, and the terrible wound he'd now borne for more than a month was left as a permanent reminder. It seemed to make even his father realize that Gregor, despite all his troubles and his terrible transformation, was nonetheless still a member of the family, who should not be treated as an enemy. On the contrary, family duty demanded they swallow their disgust and be patient, always and only patient.

His injury had probably caused him to lose his mobility for good, and it now took him forever just to get across his room, his movements like those of an ageing invalid. Crawling anywhere high up was out of the question. But to Gregor, the fact that they now left the living-room door open every evening was some compensation for his worsening condition. He looked forward eagerly to this. Lying invisible in the darkness of his room, he could see the whole family gathered round the table in the lamplight and listen freely to their conversation. This was a radical and welcome change.

It was true they no longer held those lively conversations he'd thought of longingly each time he climbed between the damp sheets of some cramped little hotel room. Most of the time, now, they sat in silence. Directly after dinner, his father would settle down to doze in his armchair, while his mother and sister hushed each other. Leaning forward into the light, his mother would sew away at some fine needlework she was doing for a clothing store, while his sister, who now worked as a sales assistant, studied shorthand and French in the hope of finding a better job. Now and then his father would wake up and, not realizing he'd been asleep, say to his wife, 'You've been sewing for so long today!' and then go straight back to sleep, prompting Gregor's mother and sister to exchange a tired smile.

Out of some obstinate whim, his father invariably refused to take off his uniform when he came back in from work. His dressing gown hung unused on the hook, and he slept in his armchair in full livery, as if to keep himself always ready to carry out the orders of his superiors, even at home. As a result, the uniform, which had not been new even when it was issued to him, grew shabbier by the day despite the best efforts of the two women. Gregor passed long evenings staring at the old man as he slept uncomfortably but peacefully in his stained and spotted jacket with its brightly polished buttons.

As soon as the clock struck ten, his mother would quietly try to rouse her husband and encourage him to go to bed, as it was impossible for him, slumped in that way, to get the sleep he needed before returning to work at six the next morning. But, with the same obstinacy that had characterized him since he'd started working at the bank, he would insist on staying at the table even though he regularly dropped off to sleep, which made it more and more difficult to coax him out of his armchair and into bed. Try as they might to urge him to move with gentle encouragements, he would sit there with his eyes tight shut for fifteen minutes at a time, slowly nodding his head and refusing to get up. Well might his wife tug him by the sleeve and whisper sweet nothings in his ear, or his daughter lay her work aside to try and help. Nothing had any effect. The old man would simply sink deeper into his chair.

Only when the two women seized him under the arms would he open his eyes, gaze at each of them in turn and say, 'What a life! Is this the hard-earned rest of my old age?' and, leaning on the two women, haul himself up as if he weighed a ton and let himself be led to the door. Once there he would wave them away and continue alone, while his wife put down her needle, his daughter her pen and they both ran fussing after him. Who in this overworked and overtired family had time to attend to Gregor, except when it came to his most pressing needs?

The household budget dwindled to the point where they had to dismiss the maid. In her place, they took on a gigantic charwoman with bony features and white hair floating around her head to come in morning and evening to do the heavy work. His mother had to take care of everything else on top of her interminable needlework. His mother and sister even had to sell off some of the family jewellery they'd worn with so much pride on high days and holidays, as Gregor discovered one evening when he heard them discussing the prices they hoped to get. But the biggest complaint was always about the flat, which was much larger than they needed and which they now found too expensive to maintain. They couldn't leave, they said, because they couldn't think of any way of moving Gregor. In fact, Gregor knew he wasn't really what stopped them from moving; they could easily have transported him in a large wooden box pierced with a few air holes. The thing that really stopped them moving was their own despair, and the sense that they had been afflicted with a misfortune unlike any that had ever before occurred in their family or circle of acquaintance.

They were now under the cosh of crushing poverty: his father had to fetch breakfast for the bank underlings; his mother worked herself to the bone mending the linen of strangers; his sister ran about behind her counter at her customers' beck and call, until the whole family was at the end of its tether.

When his mother and sister came back from putting his father to bed, laid their work down and drew their chairs close until they were sitting almost cheek to cheek, Gregor would feel the wound in his back starting to hurt again. And then pointing at Gregor's bedroom, his mother would say, 'Close the door, Grete,' and he would once again be left in the darkness, while next door the two women either mingled their tears or sat dry-eyed, staring at the table.

For long days and nights Gregor could not sleep. Sometimes he thought that the next time they opened the door, he would find himself managing his family's affairs as he always had done. Much later, his boss, the manager, the clerks and the firm's apprentices bubbled up to the surface of his mind: the nitwit office boy, two or three friends from other firms, a chambermaid in a provincial hotel – a sweet, if fleeting memory – a till girl in a hat shop he'd courted seriously but too slowly. They all paraded through his thoughts, jumbled up with strangers and long forgotten faces. But none of them could help either Gregor or his family, and he was glad when they all vanished.

He found he now no longer cared what happened to his family; on the contrary, he felt nothing but a sort of blind rage at the way they now neglected him; and even though there was no longer anything he fancied,

he began to concoct elaborate plans for a raid on the larder, with a view to taking the food to which he was still entitled, even if he wasn't hungry.

Nowadays his sister no longer took the trouble to think of something he might like to eat. She shoved any old food in with her foot before hurrying off to work in the morning and at midday. In the evening, without even bothering to see whether he'd touched his meal or not – usually, he hadn't – she would sweep away the leftovers with a whisk of the broom.

As for cleaning his room, which she now did in the evenings, she could hardly have done it any faster. Great patches of dirt streaked the wall, and little heaps of dust and rubbish lay all over the place. At first, Gregor would position himself in the filthiest places when she appeared as a kind of reproach. But even if he'd stayed there for weeks at a time, it still wouldn't have changed anything: Grete saw the dirt as well as he did, but she'd made up her mind to ignore it. Showing the same oversensitivity that had now infected them all, none of this stopped her from taking more jealous care than ever to ensure that no one else should presume on her sole right to clean the room.

One day Gregor's mother, though, took it upon herself to give Gregor's room a thorough clean. This required several buckets of water. Crouched on his sofa in bitter immobility, the ensuing deluge upset Gregor deeply; but his mother soon had her punishment. No sooner had his sister arrived home that night and noticed the difference in Gregor's room than, feeling deeply offended, she ran into the living-room and, ignoring her mother's pleading, uplifted hands, burst into a

flood of tears, which her parents – her father was frightened out of his chair – at first watched in helpless amazement. Gradually, she began to calm down. But then her father lost his temper, too. On the one hand, he began reproaching his wife for not leaving the care and cleaning of Gregor's room to Grete; on the other, he yelled at his daughter, insisting she would never again be allowed to go in and clean it. His wife tried to draw her husband, who was quite beside himself, into his bedroom. Wracked with sobs, Grete banged on the table with her little fists, while Gregor hissed loudly with rage at the idea that no one had the decency or consideration to close the door and spare him the sight of all these tear-floods and sigh-tempests.

But even if his sister, tired out by her work, could no longer be bothered to look after Gregor as diligently as before, there was no need for her mother to take up the task or for him to be neglected: they had a cleaning lady now. This elderly widow, whose big, bony frame had helped her out of worse trouble during her long life, could not really be said to feel any disgust for Gregor. One day, without being in the least curious, she opened his door. Gregor began scurrying about in alarm, although she made no move to chase him. Perfectly astonished at the sight, she froze, hands folded over her stomach.

From that moment on, she never failed morning and evening to open the door a little and peep in on him. At first she would call him over in a familiar tone with expressions like: 'Come on, you old dung beetle!' or, 'Hey, look at the old cockroach!' Gregor ignored her. He would stay motionless beneath his sofa as if no one was there. If only they'd told the

woman to clean his room out every day, instead of allowing her to go on teasing and upsetting him when the mood took her!

Early one morning, when heavy rain – perhaps a sign of approaching spring – beat on the rooftops, the old woman's taunts annoyed Gregor so much he began to turn, feebly and slowly, as if about to attack her. She was not in the least bit frightened. A chair stood by the door. She snatched it up and brandished it high in the air, opening her mouth wide: it was obvious she didn't intend closing it until she had brought the chair crashing down on Gregor's back. 'Is that it, then?' she asked, as he turned away, and she calmly put the chair back in the corner.

By this time, Gregor was hardly eating. Only when he happened on his scraps would he amuse himself by taking a piece of food in his mouth, keeping it there for hours but almost always spitting it out again. At first he thought it was his dejection over the state of his room that had made him lose his appetite, but in fact he quickly grew used to the changes. His family had fallen into the habit of throwing anything unwanted in there, and there was a great deal of this lumber now that one of the bedrooms had been let to three lodgers.

These earnest men – all three had full beards, as Gregor saw one day when he was peering through a crack in the door – were fanatically tidy. They insisted on order, not only in their own room, but also, once they were paying rent, throughout the whole flat, especially the kitchen. They had no time for useless, dirty junk. They had brought most of the things they needed with them, leaving a lot of stuff that couldn't be sold but that no one wanted to throw out. It was all chucked into Gregor's room,

along with the ash bucket and the kitchen rubbish bin. The charwoman, always in a tearing hurry, dumped anything else that looked as if it might not be needed in there too.

Luckily, all Gregor usually saw was a hand flourishing the object in question before the door slammed shut again. Perhaps the cleaner intended retrieving it all when she got the time and the opportunity; perhaps she meant to throw the whole lot out in one go. But the reality was that the rubbish remained where it had first landed, unless Gregor disturbed it as he wandered through it – at first because he had to and then later because he enjoyed it. Even so, these excursions left him half dead with fatigue, and after them he sat without moving for hours.

As the lodgers sometimes also took their dinner in the living-room, its door was occasionally closed. But Gregor no longer cared. For some time now, even when his family left the door open he'd squat back in the darkest corner of his room, unnoticed and out of sight. One day the cleaner left the dining-room door standing slightly ajar, and it was still in that position when the lodgers came in and turned on the lights. They sat down in the places that had once been occupied by Gregor, his father and his mother, unfolded their napkins and took up their knives and forks.

Gregor's mother appeared in the doorway shortly afterwards with a plate of meat, followed immediately by his sister carrying a dish piled high with potatoes. The food sent up a great cloud of steam. The lodgers leaned over as if to examine it, and the one who was seated in the middle and appeared to have some authority over the others cut a piece of meat

to see whether it was tender enough, or if he should send it back to the kitchen. He appeared satisfied, however, and the two women, who had been watching anxiously, breathed a sigh of relief. The family itself ate in the kitchen. Nevertheless, Gregor's father always came in, bowed once, and made the rounds of the table cap in hand before going back into the kitchen. The boarders rose as one, muttering something into their beards. Once they were alone, they ate in almost total silence. Gregor found it odd that he could hear the sound of their chewing over and above the clatter of the cutlery; it was as if they wanted to show him that you needed real teeth to eat properly, and that even with the finest toothless jaws in the world there was no chance of getting anything down. 'I am hungry,' thought Gregor sadly, 'but not for that kind of food. Look how those lodgers shovel it in, while I lie here wasting away.'

This whole weary time, he could not remember hearing his sister play her violin. But this evening, he heard music coming from the kitchen. The lodgers had just finished their meal; the middle one had produced a newspaper, handing a page of it to each of the others; now they were all three reading, leaning back in their chairs and smoking. The sound of the violin caught their attention, and they rose and tiptoed toward the hall door, where they halted in a tight group. Apparently, they had been heard in the kitchen: Gregor's father called, 'Does the violin upset you gentlemen? If so, we'll stop it immediately.' 'On the contrary,' the middle lodger said. 'Wouldn't the young lady like to come through and play to us here in the dining-room, where it is much nicer and more comfortable?' 'Oh, thank you,' said Mr Samsa as if he were the one playing.

The gentlemen walked back across the room and waited. Soon Gregor's father came in with the music stand, his mother with the sheets of music, and his sister with the violin. She calmly prepared to play. Her parents, who had never before let their rooms, treated the lodgers with exaggerated politeness and didn't dare sit in their own chairs. Mr Samsa leaned against the door, his right hand thrust between two buttons of his jacket. One of the gentlemen offered Gregor's mother a chair, and she sat exactly where he had placed it, off in the corner.

Gregor's sister began to play, while her father and mother, who were to either side, watched her hands as they moved over the instrument. Drawn by the music, Gregor had crawled forward a little and poked his head into the room. He was no longer surprised that he'd lost all consideration for others, the very consideration that once had been his pride and joy. Yet he had never had more reason to remain hidden: for now, as a result of all the dust in his room which flew up at the slightest disturbance, he was always covered in threads, hair and morsels of stale food, which stuck to his back and sides and trailed after him wherever he went. His apathy was now so great he no longer bothered turning on his back and rubbing himself clean on the carpet. And despite being in this filthy state, he had no qualms about crawling forward over the spotless floor.

So far, no one had noticed him. His family was wrapped up in the violin recital. Hands in their pockets, the lodgers, who had at first gathered round the music stand so that they could read the notes – putting Grete off her playing – soon moved back to the window, where they stood with

their heads down talking in low tones, watched anxiously by Mr Samsa who stood nearby.

It was perfectly clear that they were disappointed in their expectations of a fine or at least amusing recital, were fed up with the whole thing and only tolerated this interruption to their peace and quiet out of politeness. Even the snooty way they blew cigar smoke out through their noses and mouths showed how unimpressed they were.

And yet Grete was playing so beautifully. Head tilted to one side, her gaze followed the score with sorrowful care. Gregor crawled a little further forward and lowered his head in an effort to catch her eye. Was he really just an animal when music stirred him so deeply? It seemed to him to open a pathway toward that unknown source of sustenance for which he so longed.

He resolved to creep up to his sister and tug at her dress, to make her understand that she must bring her violin into his room, for no one valued her playing as he did. He would never again let her out of his room – at least, not while he lived – and for once his horrible shape would come in useful. He would be at all the doors at once, keeping all intruders at bay with his fearsome hissing. There would be no question of force; his sister must live with him of her own accord. She would sit with him on the sofa and listen to what he said. He would tell her in confidence that, had this misfortune not so swiftly overtaken him, he had planned on telling everyone last Christmas – was Christmas really past? – that he was sending her to the Conservatory, whatever anyone said.

Moved by this explanation, his sister would surely weep pure tears of happiness, and Gregor, climbing up on her shoulder, would kiss her neck; this would be all the easier, for she had worn neither collar nor ribbon since starting work in the shop.

'Mr Samsa!' cried the middle lodger. Wordlessly, he pointed his index finger at Gregor, who was advancing slowly into the room. Grete stopped playing. The middle lodger turned to his friends, grinned, shook his head and then looked back at Gregor. At first, Gregor's father seemed more concerned with reassuring the lodgers than with driving his son from the room. But the lodgers didn't seem all that upset by the spectacle: if anything, they found Gregor more entertaining than the violin. Mr Samsa hurried forward and, with outstretched arms, tried to guide them back into their room, while hiding Gregor from their eyes with his bulk. At this, they started to get annoyed, although it wasn't clear whether this was because of their landlord's behaviour or because, unwittingly, they had all been living right next door to a monster like Gregor.

Demanding Mr Samsa explain matters, they began waving their arms in the air, fiddling with their beards as they fell slowly back towards their room. In the meantime, Grete had recovered from this sudden and distressing interruption of her recital. After standing for a moment not knowing what to do – with the violin and bow dangling limply from her hands, and following the score as if she were still playing – she suddenly came back to life. She laid the violin in her mother's lap – Mrs Samsa was gasping for breath in her chair, lungs working overtime – and rushed through into the next room, towards which the lodgers were retreating

ever more rapidly in the face of Mr Samsa's advance. Pillows and blankets flew under Grete's quick, practised hands as she set their beds to rights, and she had slipped out again before they came in.

Once again in the grip of his strange obstinacy, Mr Samsa had quite forgotten the respect due his lodgers. He kept pushing them back, until the middle lodger reached the door of his room, where he stopped dead and stamped hard on the floor. 'I hereby wish to inform you,' he said, raising a hand and letting his gaze sweep the two women, 'that in view of the disgusting circumstances prevailing in this family and this house' – at this he spat contemptuously on the floor – 'as of tomorrow morning, I am giving up my room. Naturally, you will not get a penny for the time I have been living here. On the contrary, I am seriously considering whether to sue you, given how easy the case would be to prove. I shall certainly look into the matter, believe me, sir.' He broke off and stared into space as if waiting for something. His two friends spoke up in their turn: 'We, too, give our notice.' At this, the middle lodger seized the door handle, and all three trooped inside.

The door slammed shut with a bang. Gregor's father staggered over to his armchair, rested his trembling hands on the arms, and stretched out as if he were settling in for his customary evening nap; but the rapid and apparently uncontrollable nodding of his head told a very different story.

All this time, Gregor had stuck fast on the spot where he had surprised the lodgers. The disappointment over the failure of his plans, combined perhaps also with the weakness of extreme hunger, meant he could not move a muscle. He feared some terrible catastrophe would befall him at any moment and stood there waiting for the axe to descend. Even the violin didn't startle him as it slipped from his mother's trembling fingers, fell off her lap and hit the floor with a hollow sound.

'My dear parents,' said his sister, beating the table with her hand to get their attention, 'things can't go on like this. Even if you don't see it, it's clear as day to me. I won't mention my brother's name in the same breath as this monster. All I have to say is that we must find some way of getting rid of it. We've done everything humanly possible to care for it and put up with it. No one can say that we're to blame.'

'She's right, a thousand times right,' her father said. But her mother, who still hadn't got her breath back, coughed into her hand with a wild look. Her daughter hurried over to her and held her forehead. Grete's words seemed to have made up her father's mind: he sat up and poked at his cap, which was lying on the table among the dishes left from the lodgers' dinner. From time to time he stared at Gregor.

'We must find a way of getting rid of it,' she repeated, now speaking only to her father. Her mother's coughing was making her deaf. 'It'll be the death of you both, I can see it coming. When people have to work all day, like us, they can't put up with constant torture at home. I certainly can't.' And she wept so bitterly that her tears, wiped mechanically away, fell on her mother's face. 'But what can we do, child?' her father said, demonstrating remarkable grasp and compassion. Grete merely shrugged her shoulders, as if to show that the confusion brought on by her emotional state had banished her former self-assurance. 'If only he could

understand us,' her father said wonderingly. But Grete signalled through her tears that this was out of the question.

'If only he could understand us,' her father said again – and he shut his eyes as he spoke, as if to show that he agreed with Grete that such a thing was quite impossible. 'If only he could understand us, then perhaps we could come to some accommodation with him. But as it is...'

'That thing has to go!' Grete cried. 'It's the only way, Father. You have to stop believing it's Gregor. We've believed that for far too long, that's why we're so unhappy. How could it be Gregor? If it were really him, he would have realized long since that he can't possibly live with human beings and would have left of his own free will. I no longer have a brother – but what we can do is go on living and respect his memory. Instead, this monster dogs our footsteps, drives our lodgers away and schemes to take over the whole flat. We'll be out on the streets, soon! Look, Father, look!' she screamed suddenly, 'He's off again!' And in a panic Gregor couldn't begin to understand, she jumped out of her chair, abandoning Mrs Samsa as if she would rather throw her own mother to the four winds than be anywhere near Gregor. She ran behind her father. Deeply upset by her behaviour, he stood up and spread his arms wide to protect her.

But Gregor had no desire to frighten anyone, least of all his sister. He had merely started to turn around in order to go back into his room. Given that in his weakened state Gregor had to keep bumping his head on the floor to help push himself around, this looked very peculiar. He stopped and looked back at them. They seemed to realize he meant well; the momentary panic had passed. They watched him in silent sorrow.

Mrs Samsa lay back in her armchair, legs outstretched and pressed tightly together, eyelids drooping with fatigue. Grete sat beside her father with her arm around his neck. 'Now perhaps I can turn around,' Gregor thought, bending again to the task. He couldn't stop himself from wheezing loudly, and he was forced to rest from time to time. But no one hurried him, they left him to get on with it. His turn completed, he beat a hasty retreat. He was amazed at the great distance that now seemed to separate him from his bedroom.

Weak as he now felt, he couldn't understand how he had only recently covered the same ground with so little effort. Focused wholly on regaining his room, he failed to notice that his family hadn't uttered a single word between them. It was only when he had at long last reached his door that he thought of turning his head – not completely, because his neck had become very stiff – but enough to see that nothing behind him had changed. His sister was the only one standing. He reserved his last glance for his mother who by now was fast asleep.

The second he was back in his room someone slammed, locked and double-bolted the door. The loud, sudden crash from behind made Gregor's legs buckle in fright. It was his sister who had rushed to the door. She'd been standing ready, and at the right moment had raced forward on her toes so that he couldn't hear her. As she turned the key in the lock, she glanced back at her parents and cried, 'At last!'

'Now what?' Gregor wondered, peering round in the darkness. He soon discovered that he was unable to move. This didn't surprise him in the least: it seemed to him much more remarkable that his frail little legs had

supported him up until now. But on the whole he felt quite comfortable. It was true that his whole body ached, but these pains seemed gradually to be fading away. By now he hardly felt the rotten apple in his back, or the inflamed, dust-covered area surrounding it. He thought tenderly and lovingly of his family. He knew he had to go; he was even more certain of it than his sister had been. He lay dreaming in a half-trance until the church clock struck three in the morning. He watched the world growing lighter through the window. Then, without his willing it, his head drooped and a last feeble breath left his nostrils in a soft stream.

The cleaner arrived early in the morning. Although she had often been asked not to do so, she slammed all the doors so loudly in her hustle and bustle that once she was in the house it was impossible to remain asleep. At first, she didn't notice anything out of the ordinary as she paid Gregor her usual quick morning visit. She thought he was lying motionless on purpose, feigning injury. She gave him every credit for intelligence. She had a long broom in her hand, and tried to tickle him from the doorway. When there was still no response she grew irritated and poked him a couple of times. It was only when this, too, failed to budge him that the truth hit her.

Grasping what had happened, she opened her eyes wide and whistled in astonishment. At once, she ran to the bedroom door and wrenched it open, shouting out into the darkness, 'Come and look! It's stone dead! It's lying there, absolutely dead as a doornail!'

Mr and Mrs Samsa sat up in bed. The cleaner had frightened them so much they could not at first make sense of her words. But now they

hastily scrambled out of bed, Mr Samsa on one side, his wife on the other. Mr Samsa threw the quilt over his shoulders, while Mrs Samsa came out clad in nothing but her nightdress and they hurried into Gregor's room. Meanwhile, Grete had opened the living-room door. She had been sleeping there ever since the lodgers arrived. She was fully dressed, and the pallor of her skin suggested she hadn't slept a wink. 'Dead?' said Mrs Samsa, shooting the cleaner a questioning look, even though she could see perfectly well for herself what had happened. 'I should say so,' the cleaner replied, giving Gregor's corpse a hefty shove with her broom to prove it. Mrs Samsa made as if to stop her, but then faltered. 'Well,' Mr Samsa said, 'let's all thank God for that!' He crossed himself and the three women followed his example. Grete, whose eyes had never once left the corpse, said, 'Look how thin he was! It was such a long time since he'd eaten anything. The food came out of his room exactly as it went in.' Gregor's body was indeed quite flat and dry – they could only see this clearly now that his legs had collapsed, and there was nothing to distract them. 'Come in our room for a minute, Grete,' Mrs Samsa said with a sad smile, and Grete followed her parents into their bedroom, glancing continually back at the corpse as she went.

The cleaner shut the door and threw the window wide open. Despite the early hour, the fresh morning air held a certain warmth. It was already the end of March. The three lodgers came out of their room and cast round in astonishment for their breakfast, but everyone had forgotten them. 'Where's our breakfast?' the middle lodger asked the cleaner grumpily. But she put a finger to her lips and urged them silently to follow her to Gregor's bedroom.

They went in and stood around the corpse, hands in the pockets of their rather shabby coats, in the middle of a room already brilliant with sunlight. Then the bedroom door opened and Mr Samsa appeared in his uniform, with his wife on one side and his daughter on the other. They all looked as if they had been crying, and now and again Grete pressed her face against her father's arm.

'Leave my house immediately!' Mr Samsa barked, pointing to the door while holding on tight to his family.

'Whatever do you mean?' said the middle lodger with a timid smile, somewhat taken aback. The two others kept their hands behind their backs, rubbing the palms together as if looking forward to a row that must surely end in their favour. 'I mean exactly what I say!' Mr Samsa retorted, marching directly at the middle lodger and his companions. The lodger stood his ground, eyes fixed on the floor, as if he were contemplating the changed circumstances. 'Very well then, we'll go,' he said at last, raising his eyes to Mr Samsa as if, in a sudden access of humility, he sought approval for his words. Mr Samsa did no more than nod, glaring. At this, the principal lodger strode out into the hallway, his two friends – their hands now quite still – scurrying after him as if they were afraid Mr Samsa might get there before them and cut them off. In the hallway, they took their hats from the pegs, lifted their walking sticks from the umbrella stand, bowed silently and quit the apartment.

FRANZ KAFKA

With a mistrust that was self-evidently and wholly unjustified, Mr Samsa and his wife and daughter followed the three men out on to the landing and leaned over the balustrade to watch as they slowly but steadily descended the long staircase, appearing and disappearing as they spiralled downwards floor by floor. The farther they went down, the more the Samsas lost interest, and when the lodgers had met and passed a butcher's boy climbing proudly up the stairs with his basket on his head, the family turned from the railing and went back indoors with a sigh of relief.

They decided to spend the remainder of the day resting and strolling. They not only deserved the break, they very much needed it. And so they sat down at the table to write three letters of apology: Mr Samsa to the bank manager, Mrs Samsa to her employer and Grete to her boss. While they were writing, the cleaner came in to say that she'd finished her work and was leaving. At first, the Samsas merely nodded without raising their eyes; it was only when the cleaner showed no signs of actually going that they looked crossly up at her. 'Well?' Mr Samsa demanded. The cleaner was standing in the doorway, smiling as if she had some good news, but would only spit it out if they questioned her in the right way. The little ostrich feather sticking up out of her hat, which had annoyed Mr Samsa from the moment she'd started cleaning for them, bobbed about merrily all over the place. Mrs Samsa, whom the cleaner had always respected the most asked, 'What is it?' 'What I wanted to say,' the woman replied, laughing so much she could hardly get the words out, 'is that you needn't worry about getting rid of that rubbish next door. I've already taken care of it.' Grete and her mother bent back to the table as if to resume their letter-writing. Realizing that the woman was about to launch into a more detailed explanation, Mr Samsa cut her short with a peremptory gesture. Cut off in mid-sentence, the cleaner suddenly remembered that she was in a great hurry and, calling, 'Goodbye, everyone,' in a furious voice, she turned on her heel and disappeared, slamming the door behind her with an almighty crash.

'This evening we must sack her,' Mr Samsa declared. But neither his wife nor his daughter replied. Even the cleaner had not been able to disturb their newfound tranquillity. The two of them rose, went to the window and stood there with their arms around each other. Turning towards them in his armchair, Mr Samsa stared over for a moment in silence. Then he said, 'Well, well, it's all water under the bridge now. So you can start paying me some attention.' The women hurried across to him, kissed him and finished off their letters as quickly as possible. Then they all left the apartment together, something they hadn't done for months, and took the tram out to the countryside.

There were no other passengers in the compartment, which was warm and bright in the sunlight. Leaning comfortably back in their seats, they fell to discussing the future. On closer examination, they decided things weren't nearly as bad as they'd imagined. The fact was – and this was something they hadn't really discussed among themselves before – that they'd all three found reasonable jobs, which promised even better for the future. The greatest immediate improvement they could make to their circumstances was to move from their current apartment to a smaller, cheaper and more practical

flat, and above all a place in a much better neighbourhood than the one Gregor had chosen for them.

As their daughter grew more and more animated, Mr and Mrs Samsa realized almost as one that, despite all the terrible things she'd been through over these past weeks which had left her looking so pale and wan, Grete was blossoming into a beautiful, full-figured young woman.

They fell quiet, and communicating via little more than meaningful glances, they both saw that the time had come to find her a good husband. And when, at the end of the journey, their daughter stood and stretched her young body before them, it came almost as a confirmation of their new hopes and dreams.

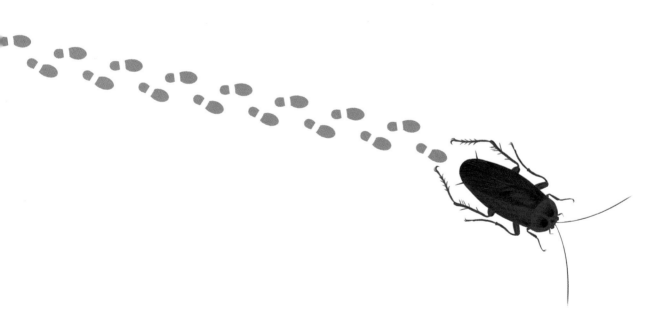